King
Max

King Max

by Dick King-Smith

illustrated by Brian Floca

Chapter 1

"There's one!" said the man with the flashlight. "Get him!"

The man with the net tossed it neatly over the hurrying hedgehog. Although neither of the men could know this, they had in fact caught a most unusual hedgehog—none other than Victor Maximilian St. George, known to his family as Max.

Some time ago, while trying to find a way for hedgehogs to cross busy roads safely, Max had been hit by a passing bicyclist. This accident had caused him to muddle his words. So that, as he told his family, "Something bot me on the

hittom, and then I headed my bang. My ache bads headly." For quite a while after that, he had considered himself to be a hodgeheg.

A second bump on the head had restored Max's mind to normal, and soon after he had succeeded in his task and had thus become something of a hero to hedgehogkind.

But now, on this particular evening, he felt anything but heroic as the net dropped over him. He rolled himself into a tight ball, his heart hammering in fright.

"Put him in this sack," said the man with the flashlight.

"Okay," said the man with the net. "He's not all that old, judging by his size. He'll do nicely."

Max's family lived in the garden of Number 5A in a row of suburban houses. When dawn broke, they were concerned.

"Ma! Pa! Max hasn't come home!" squeaked his three sisters, Peony, Pansy, and Petunia.

"Don't worry," said Ma Hedgehog. But she did.

"He'll be back any minute," said Pa. But Max wasn't.

From Number 5B next door, the neighbor poked his head through the hedge. He was an elderly bachelor hedgehog who was fond of Ma and Pa's children. They called him Uncle B.

"What's up?" asked Uncle B. "Is something wrong?"

"Max hasn't come home," said Pa. "He went across to the Park last evening, hunting. He hasn't returned."

"He probably decided to stay there and get a good day's sleep," said Uncle B. in a comforting voice.

"But suppose . . . ?" said Ma, and then she stopped.

"No, no," said Uncle B. "Don't even think about it. If there's one hedgehog in the world that knows all about road safety, it's young Max."

♛

Young Max was, at that very moment, sitting in a wire cage in a laboratory at the local university. The scientists who had captured him—their names were Dandy-Green and Duck—were doing a study of hedgehog behavior, and they needed to learn as much as possible about the creatures' nightlife.

"Now," said Dr. Dandy-Green, "first we'll fit him with a radio collar."

"And then we can follow his movements," said Professor Duck.

But that was easier said than done, they found.

To begin with, when they opened the cage door and (with gloves on) lifted Max out, he rolled himself up. And even if he hadn't, they realized, fitting a collar on a hedgehog is an impossible task. For starters, a hedgehog has no neck to speak of, and anyway, there's no way of getting any sort of collar to stay on, on top of all those prickles.

They put Max back in the cage.

"It's hopeless," said Professor Duck. "We might as well let him go."

"Not yet," said Dr. Dandy-Green. "Maybe we'll think of something."

So they sat and thought.

Max sat and thought, too. Where was he? What was this place? Who were these men? Why had they caught him? What was to become of him? How he longed to be back at Number 5A with Ma and Pa and Peony and Pansy and Petunia and good old Uncle B. next door.

Thinking of Uncle B. reminded him that the men had put a bowl of Munchimeat dog food (the old hedgehog's favorite) in the cage. *There's no point in starving to death,* Max said to himself, and he began to nibble at the food.

"He's eating," said the doctor.

"Yes," said the professor. "He's a healthy young animal. It's a shame we can't use him."

"You haven't thought of any way to attach a transmitter to him?"

"No. I'm afraid not. I'm completely stuck."

"Stuck . . . ?" said Dr. Dandy-Green. "Stuck! That's it!"

"What's what?" asked Professor Duck.

"That's the way to attach the transmitter. Stick it to him!"

"With glue?"

"Yes! Stick it to the spines on the back of his head. Then we can locate him wherever he is."

"That's brilliant!" said the professor. "And how about this? We could fit him with a little flashing light. We'll run it off the same batteries. Then we can spot him in the dark."

"Great idea!" said the doctor.

They stood up and stared into Max's cage.

Max stared back.

"I wonder what he's thinking?" said Dr. Dandy-Green.

"He's probably wishing he was back home with his family," said Professor Duck.

I wish I was back home with my family, thought Max.

"He will be," said the doctor.

"As soon as we've got him ready," said the professor. "When we're done, he's going to be a very unusual hedgehog."

Chapter 2

When a couple of days had gone by with no sight of Max, the family at Number 5A had almost given up hope of ever seeing him again. Ma was convinced he had been run over, even though Pa and Uncle B. had checked all the local roads and reported no squashings. Peony, Pansy, and Petunia, who were romantic girls, thought Max had fallen in love and was busy courting. They whispered and giggled a lot together.

Pa decided that Max had simply left home to seek his fortune in the wide world.

"Didn't even bother to say good-bye," he grumbled.

Uncle B. said nothing, but he was sad, for he was especially fond of Max. He searched the Park from end to end—in the Ornamental Gardens, around the Bandstand, and beside the Lily Pond—and met a number of hedgehogs searching for food but found no sign of his young friend.

Meanwhile, the scientists' plans were coming along. They had prepared a very small battery-powered radio transmitter and had mounted a little electric lamp on top of it. The lamp revolved—like the beam of a lighthouse—throwing out a blue light.

Now all they had to do was attach it to Max.

This turned out to be easier than they had expected, especially because Max had by now become used to them and no longer rolled up when they touched him.

They smeared glue on the base of the transmitter and over the spines on the back of Max's neck. Then, while Max was busy with his Munchimeat, they were able to press the

two surfaces together long enough for the glue to set.

"How about that?" said Dr. Dandy-Green.

"Excellent," said Professor Duck. "It looks as if he's wearing a crown."

"Other hedgehogs will be impressed, especially when his little light is flashing," said Dr. Dandy-Green. "Between that and the transmitter, we'll be able to follow him wherever he goes."

As for Max, he hardly noticed the device, for it weighed very little, and, placed as it was, there was no way he could actually see it. All he thought about was freedom. He was glad to be well fed, but he was also fed up.

He would have been very happy if he could have understood what was said next.

"When should we release him?" said Dr. Dandy-Green.

"How about tomorrow evening?" replied Professor Duck. "After we've tested the equipment?"

"Okay. Where shall we release him?"

"In that park where we caught him, I think. That's probably his home territory."

"He should have a name or number or something," said the doctor.

"Yes," agreed the professor. "When we're taking notes on his movements, we don't want to have to write 'the hedgehog did this or that' every time."

They looked at Victor Maximilian St. George, wearing (although he did not know it) his crown.

"We need something short," said Dr. Dandy-Green.

"How about 'E.E.'?" said Professor Duck.

"E.E.?"

"Yes. The initials of his Latin name, *Erinaceus europaeus*."

"E.E. it is!"

The next day they tested all of their equipment, allowing Max to trot around the laboratory floor and up and down the corridors while they took turns holding the receiver and following him. Everything worked perfectly.

The transmitter transmitted, the receiver received, and the flashing light flashed.

This last thing puzzled Max, since he could not see where the intermittent blue light was coming from, but he soon grew used to it. He was disappointed to be put back into his cage, but then, that evening, he left it for good.

What happened next is best described by the notes that Professor Duck and Dr. Dandy-Green wrote up the following day.

10:30 P.M. Took E.E. to Park, released him beside Bandstand. E.E. raised snout, scented air, set off NNW across Park toward nearest road, traveling fast. This route took him around the Lily Pond and through the Ornamental Gardens, where it was not easy to observe his light in dense shrubs, flower beds, etc., and radio contact was needed. In open areas E.E.'s light was easily visible. Became nervous when E.E. arrived at road, since evening traffic was still somewhat busy. Astonished to observe E.E. waiting patiently at curbside until road was completely clear. E.E. then looked left, looked right, looked left again, and calmly crossed, revolving light flashing. Fortunately, this phenomenon was observed by Prof. D. and Dr. D-G. only. E.E. then went under a gate (Number 5A) and into a suburban garden. Looking over garden wall, Prof. D. and Dr. D-G. saw several hedgehogs, which all fled as E.E. approached. Continued observation, however, revealed that these animals (two adults and three juveniles) returned cautiously after a while and were then joined by another adult from the garden of Number 5B. Much squeaking and grunting and many coughlike snorts were heard. Waited some time, but E.E. seemed unwilling to move, so discontinued observation at 11:43 P.M.

The family at Number 5A had been quietly snail hunting in the rock garden when suddenly under the gate had come the strangest apparition. It looked like Max, it smelled like Max, but what was that object on its head, and what was that ugly blue light that flickered around and around and lit them up one after the other? For an instant they froze in terror, and then Ma squealed, "It's his ghost! It's Max's ghost. He's come to haunt us!" and they all ran for cover.

Max stood in the middle of the lawn and called, "Ma! Pa! Girls! It's only me. I'm home."

Pa was the first one out of the flower bed. He approached Max cautiously, blinking each time the blue flashes passed over him.

"Is it really you, son?" he asked.

"Yes, Pa."

"What's that thing on your head?"

"I can't see it, Pa," Max said.

Peony, Pansy, and Petunia came forward.

"Oo!" they squeaked. "Look at Max's hat! It's so pretty! Can we get hats like that, Ma?"

Ma nervously shuffled nearer.

"Oh, Max!" she said. "What's happened to you?"

Max was about to tell them all about being captured by the two men and put in a cage, but just then Uncle B. came pushing through the hedge. He saw Max and stopped dead in his tracks.

"Oh, no!" he said softly. "It can't be!"

"It is!" the others cried. "It's Max!"

"But can't you see what he's wearing?" said Uncle B. "Haven't you ever heard of the legend of the King?"

"What king?" they asked.

"Why," cried Uncle B., "the King of the Hedgehogs! Look at his crown of light! Your boy Max has been chosen to rule over hedgehogkind!"

Me? thought Max. *The King of the Hedgehogs, huh? I like the sound of that.*

He lowered his head so that the blue light shone more brightly upon them all.

"Bless you, my people," he said.

Chapter 3

There were many reactions to this new and so different Max.

Old Uncle B. was overcome with joy. As a very young boar he had first heard from his mother the story of the Hedgehog King who would one day appear. But he had never dreamed that he would live to see this appearance! Or that the King would be his young friend Max, of all hedgehogs! Uncle B. remembered that first adventure, when, before the astonished eyes of the crossing guard, they had all followed Max across the busy road in perfect safety.

I should have known then, thought Uncle B., *that he was destined for greatness.*

Ma was awestruck.

"I am the mother of a king," she kept repeating to herself in a daze.

Pa was puzzled. Who ever heard of a hedgehog wearing a crown—a crown, what's more, that flashed blue light? Yet here was his son, doing just that. *He's big-headed enough already,* thought Pa. *Who knows what he'll be like now that he's got all that stuff on his head, too?*

As for Peony, Pansy, and Petunia, they were thrilled. If Max was King, they knew what they must be, and they frisked around the garden, squeaking, "I'm Princess Peony!" and "I'm Princess Pansy!" and "I'm Princess Petunia!"

They were so excited that they did not see the shadowy shape approaching.

At the sight of the three young hedgehogs frolicking on the lawn, the fox stood quite still, his muzzle pointing toward them, his bushy tail straight out behind him, one forepaw raised. He loved the taste of tender young hedgehog.

He was a town fox born and raised, expert at tipping the lids off trash cans and undoing the doors of rabbit hutches, and he had also come up with a clever way of dealing with hedgehogs. Tightly curled into a ball, they were safe from most foxes, but this one had his own method (and a rather disgusting method at that) of making a hedgehog unroll. Then a quick bite to the stomach would put an end to it.

The fox moved forward, and now, seeing him and smelling him, Peony, Pansy, and Petunia hastily rolled up.

Standing above the nearest one (it was Pansy), the fox prepared to cock his leg, just like a dog on a lamppost, when suddenly Max appeared around the corner of Number 5A.

To his horror he saw a fox standing over one of his sisters.

Then, to his amazement, he saw the fox—obviously unnerved by the sight of a hedgehog wearing a crown of flashing light—dash away and leap the garden wall and disappear.

He was scared of me, thought Max. *That fox was frightened of me. That's why he ran away. And why was he frightened?*

Because of my crown of light!

Because he also thinks I'm the King of the Hedgehogs! What if I am?

"It's okay, girls," he said. "You can uncurl now. The fox has gone. I scared him off."

"Oh, Max!" cried Peony, Pansy, and Petunia. "Your Majesty! You're wonderful!"

Yes, said Max to himself, *I guess I am. Just think! King Max the First, the head of the Royal Family. Wait a minute—you can't have a family without a wife. What I need is a queen!*

"Look, girls," he said to his sisters, "you have a lot of friends around here, down the road and over in the Park, don't you?"

They giggled. "Boyfriends, you mean?" they asked.

"No, no," said Max. "I mean girls, around your own age."

Peony, Pansy, and Petunia looked at one another and tittered.

"Yes," they said. "Lots of them."

"And they're pretty?" asked Max in an offhand way.

"Some are," they said.

To humans, of course, even to skilled observers like Professor Duck and Dr. Dandy-Green, all hedgehogs look alike. Males are a little larger than females, but one animal looks much like another.

Hedgehogs themselves, however, can see all kinds of differences between individuals. The look in the eye, the pitch of the voice, the walk—all these details can make one hedgehog more attractive than another.

Max's sisters had always considered him good-looking, but now, with his crown of light, they thought he must be the handsomest hedgehog boar that ever lived. And his bride would have to be the most beautiful sow.

"Well, you can spread the word around," said Max. "I'm looking for a girlfriend."

"You mean . . . ?" said Peony, and then she stopped.

"You mean you want . . . ?" said Pansy, and then she stopped.

"You mean," said Petunia, "you want to get married?"

"Possibly," said Max in a bored voice. "Anyway, if any of your girlfriends are interested, tell them to come see me tomorrow night."

"Where?" asked Peony.

"Well, not here," said Max quickly. "Ma and Pa don't need to know anything about it, or Uncle B. They'd just start lecturing me about the importance of choosing the right wife and that kind of stuff."

"Where then?" asked Pansy.

"In the Park," said Max.

"Where in the Park?" asked Petunia.

Max thought. "At the Bandstand," he said. "There's plenty of room there, and it's sheltered if it rains. You'd better go now, so you can be back by dawn. And be careful when you cross the road."

"Okay, Your Majesty," they said, and the three little sows trotted off, giggling like crazy.

♛

The following night, Professor Duck and Dr. Dandy-Green came out with their receiver to record the movements of E.E.

They started out at Number 5A, but there was no radio contact and no sign of E.E.'s light, so they crossed to the Park and made a thorough search there. They had no success in the open spaces, or by the Lily Pond, or in the Ornamental Gardens, but as they neared the Bandstand, the receiver began to pick up signals.

Moving very quietly and cautiously, the professor and the doctor crept closer. They were rewarded by the sight of that flashing blue light. What they saw next is once again best described by their notes.

10:30 P.M. Commenced search (Prof. D. operating receiver) at Number 5A, where E.E. was last sighted. Made no contact, so proceeded to Park.

11:43 P.M. Located E.E. at Park Bandstand. Clear signals, and light was working well. Could only see E.E. at first, standing motionless in center of circular interior of Bandstand. However, light flashes revealed a number of other hedgehogs present.

12:02 A.M. Fortunately moon rose and revealed scene. At one side of circle three juveniles (females?) stood side by side (and remained there throughout proceedings), squeaking a great deal (excitement?). At other side Dr. D-G. counted fifteen hedgehogs waiting in a line *(note that this point is emphasized: no previous recorded observation of such behavior). At some signal (from E.E.?), animal at head of line moved into center of circle and walked up and*

down several times in front of E.E. (as though seeking approval: Dr. D-G. was reminded of fashion-show model on catwalk) before exiting Bandstand and disappearing. Each hedgehog in line performed similarly, parading one after the other before E.E., lit by blue flashes from E.E.'s light. E.E. watched each carefully. No way of *determining whether these animals were males or females, but none showed aggression toward E.E. as young males might have, and general behavior suggests that they were all females. Could E.E. possibly have been making a choice of mate? No sign that he did so. When last in line had left, the three juvenile spectators came forward to E.E. (Both Prof. D. and Dr. D-G. suspect these are the three juveniles observed in the garden of Number 5A the previous night, probably E.E.'s siblings.) Once again, much squeaking, grunting, and snorting occurred.*

Observation discontinued 12:55 A.M.

"Well?" cried Peony, Pansy, and Petunia excitedly. "What did you think, Max? Did you see anyone you liked?"

"A few of them weren't bad," said Max loftily. "But there wasn't anyone fit for a king."

Chapter 4

In the next-door garden, Pa and Uncle B. were chatting. Number 5A's people only ever put out bread and milk for their hedgehogs, but the people who lived in Number 5B were more thoughtful and provided Munchimeat. Uncle B. could never eat all they gave him, so there was an open invitation for Pa to come over and help him out whenever he felt like it, which was often.

Pa swallowed a final mouthful.

"Look, B.," he said. "Tell me the truth, hog to hog. Do you really believe in this Hedgehog King story?"

"Absolutely, my dear fellow," said Uncle B. "I'm just surprised that your parents never told you about the legend."

"They died when I was very young," said Pa. "Heavy truck. On the main road going out of town. Flattened both of them."

"In their death they were not divided," said Uncle B. gravely.

"Dead right," said Pa.

"How proud they would have been of their grandson, Max," said Uncle B. "Or King Max, I should say, now that we know he's the chosen one."

"King Max!" snorted Pa. "I'm never going to get used to that."

"Take it from me, my friend," said Uncle B. "Your young son is the elected ruler of hedgehogkind—it's as plain as the snout on your face. What other hedgehog has ever worn a crown that flashes blue light? We are his subjects, all of us."

At this point, Max came through a hole in the hedge that separated Numbers 5A and 5B.

"I'm starving," he said. "Any Munchimeat left?"

"No," said Pa shortly.

"Oh, sire!" cried Uncle B., blinking at the flashing light. "I should have kept some for you. Please forgive me. Let me see now—can I find you some snails? Or would Your Majesty prefer worms? Or beetles?"

"Oh, don't get your prickles in a twist," said Max rudely. "Next time, just make sure you leave me some food."

"Now look here, boy . . . !" Pa began angrily, but the King of the Hedgehogs had already trotted off.

"Max!" shouted Pa. "Stop, do you hear me? I want to talk to you." And he hurried after his son. *Rude young hog!* he said to himself. *Talking to B. like that. I'll give him a piece of my mind, king or no king.*

Max had already crossed the road and was headed for the Park gates when he heard Pa's voice. He turned around to see his father step off the curb without looking left or right. Just at that moment, a car came around the corner. The beam of its headlights fell directly upon Pa, who instantly rolled into a ball, right in the middle of the road.

"Pa!" cried Max, rushing back.

Some humans are kind and some are cruel, and it so happened that the driver of this particular car was the sort of person for whom squashing hedgehogs was fun.

Slowing down a little—for he wanted to be sure he hit his target—he steered deliberately to run over Pa.

Just then he saw, out of the corner of his eye, a light, a blue light, a flashing light, coming quickly, very low down, across the road. It was a light, what's more, that seemed to be fixed to the head of another hedgehog!

At this uncanny sight, he wrenched his steering wheel wildly. There was a loud crash as he missed Pa and hit a blue mailbox on the sidewalk.

As the driver sat, half-stunned, in his wrecked car, Pa unrolled to find his son staring anxiously at him.

"Pa! Pa! Are you all right?" cried Max.

"Of course I'm all right," growled Pa furiously. "No thanks to you. It's all your fault. I wouldn't have gone out if it hadn't

been for you and your rudeness, you young whippersnapper. Talking to your Uncle B. like that! Who do you think you are?"

I think I'm the King of the Hedgehogs, thought Max, *but perhaps I'd better not say so right now.* So he said nothing, and Pa turned and went back under the gate of Number 5A, grumbling loudly to himself.

By the time the police arrived, the driver had climbed out and was looking at his car and the mailbox, both dented, in a daze.

"What happened?" asked one of the two policemen.

"It was a hedgehog," said the driver.

"A hedgehog?"

"Well, two hedgehogs actually."

"Made you swerve, huh?" asked the other policeman.

"Yes."

"And you overdid it a bit, I'd guess."

"You would have, too," said the driver. "One of them had a light on his head."

"One of the hedgehogs?"

"Yes."

"Had a light on his head?"

"Yes. A blue flashing light," said the driver. "A revolving one." He pointed at the police car. "Just like you've got."

"I see," said the second policeman.

He looked at his partner and rolled his eyes.

"Now, why don't you just come along with us, sir? We'd like to talk to you down at the station."

Chapter 5

The scientists' notes from the next night made interesting reading.

10:39 P.M. Located E.E. near Park gates. Radio contact was excellent and light was still working well. It is now clear that possession of this flashing light has made E.E. the dominant individual among the local hedgehog community. Prof. D. and Dr. D-G. observed a number of hedgehogs approaching E.E. in what was very obviously a respectful manner, some even curling into a ball in front of him. E.E. appeared to be searching (for a mate?), but apparently without success.

11:15 P.M. A big crowd of hedgehogs (presumably both males and females), adults, juveniles, and even some very young animals, followed closely at E.E.'s heels as he crisscrossed the Park. Is this close attention inspired by E.E. as an individual? Or by his light? Or both? In any case, E.E. reacted angrily against this show of respect, and at 11:35 P.M. E.E. suddenly turned on his followers. All then moved away, as though they were obeying an order, leaving E.E. alone.

11:40 P.M. Heavy downpour of rain began, causing slugs and snails to become active. E.E. feeding greedily.

11:53 P.M. Prof. D. and Dr. D-G. discontinued observation in order to seek shelter. However, on way out of Park, at 12:00 midnight precisely, Prof.

D. noticed pale shape in shrubs at edge of Ornamental Gardens. Upon closer inspection, this proved to be an albino hedgehog, the spines white, the pupils of the eyes pink, a young, healthy animal. It was decided to test E.E.'s reaction to this unusual individual. The albino hedgehog was caught (in Dr. D-G.'s hat) and taken back to the location of the last sighting of E.E.

12:12 A.M. Albino hedgehog released in front of E.E., but it showed no signs of respect for him (weak eyesight?). E.E., however, appeared excited and interested. (Note: albino hedgehogs are unusual rather than rare; however, neither Prof. D. nor Dr. D-G. has ever encountered one. Neither, apparently, had E.E.) A great deal of squeaking and grunting occurred. Without warning, albino hedgehog attacked E.E., biting his snout and then taking off.

Observation ended 12:14 A.M.

"Ouch! That hurt!" cried Max, but there was no answer as the pale stranger hurried away.

Max felt quite sorry for himself for a moment. *What a night!* he thought. *First Pa yells at me, then I have to put up with all those hogs bowing and scraping to me ("Yes, Your Majesty! No, Your Majesty! Whatever you say, Your Majesty!"), and then a crowd of them follows me around, ruining my hunting, until I lose my temper and tell them to get lost ("Oh, we're so sorry, Your Majesty!").*

But then I thought things were beginning to improve. A little rain, a delicious bellyful of slugs and snails, and finally, this fantastic girl appears, white as snow, with lovely pink eyes! There's my queen, *I thought,* watch me impress her.

He had moved toward her confidently, his crown of light flashing on her so that her pale spines looked bluish and her eyes glistened redly. *What a beauty!* thought Max. *She's just perfect.*

"Hi there, baby!" he cried. "What do they call you?"

"My name," said the albino hedgehog in a chilly voice, "is Bianca. I am not a baby, and my mother brought me up not to speak to strange boars. So why don't you get lost?"

"Hey, hey!" said Max. "You can't talk to me like that. Don't you know who I am?"

"No," Bianca replied, "and I don't want to."

"But I'm the King of the Hedgehogs," said Max. "King Max the First, that's me. Can't you see my crown?"

"Yes," said Bianca. "It hurts my eyes. Turn it off."

I can't, thought Max.

"I don't wish to," he said, "and anyway, you

should address me as Your Majesty. But I'll forgive you, since you're so cute. Come on, Bianca, let's get together."

"We'll get together all right," said the albino hedgehog, and with that she bit Max sharply on his snout before hurrying off into the darkness.

Although Professor Duck and Dr. Dandy-Green witnessed the attack on E.E., they could not know what was going on in his mind, even as he nursed his sore and bleeding nose.

Oh, Bianca! he was thinking. *Oh, what a girl! What beauty! And what spirit!*

The two scientists could not possibly have understood that Victor Maximilian St. George was head over heels in love.

Chapter 6

The arrival of the palely beautiful Bianca caused great excitement among the young hedgehog boars who lived in the Park and the surrounding neighborhood. None of them had ever seen a hedgehog quite like her, and all of them were very attracted.

To Max's great annoyance, many of them began to follow her around. What if she chose one of them as her mate? Max couldn't stand the thought of it.

He summoned Peony, Pansy, and Petunia.

"Pass the word," he said to them. "All young male hedgehogs must come to a meeting tonight. In the Bandstand. By order of the King."

"All young males?" asked Peony.

"Why?" said Pansy.

"Can we come to the meeting?" asked Petunia.

"Of course not," said Max. "Go on now, get moving."

"Okay, Sire," they squeaked, and they ran away, giggling as usual.

By now there wasn't a hedgehog in the area that dared to disobey the King, so the Bandstand was packed that evening. Once again Max placed himself in the center of the circular interior, the flashes from his revolving light playing upon the faces of the audience.

No one noticed the two humans, one holding a receiver, who stood silent in the darkness beyond the Bandstand.

"I have called you here tonight," said Max in what he thought was a regal voice, "to express my displeasure at the behavior of some of you toward a newcomer to our Park, a newcomer, I may say, of a different color."

"Bianca!" someone murmured softly.

"She has not been treated with proper respect," said Max, "and I have no doubt she is upset by your unwanted attentions. These attentions will cease, as of now. Is that clearly understood?"

"Yes, Your Majesty," said a number of grudging voices, and Max swept out of the Bandstand in what he thought was a regal manner.

The scientists' notes the next day recorded the gathering:

9:42 P.M. Large number of hedgehogs assembled within Bandstand. E.E. stood at center. Much grunting from E.E., who then departed. As soon as he had gone (9:58 P.M.), remaining hedgehogs burst out in loud chorus of squeaks, squeals, snorts, and grunts,

which continued until 10:02 P.M.
Animals angry (perhaps at E.E.)?

Once Max had left the Bandstand, a babble of voices arose.

"That's it, guys. We're out of it."

"The King wants her for himself, I'll bet."

"Well, she'll make a beautiful Queen."

"She is pretty, isn't she?"

"Talk about a sweetheart!"

"Those pale spines!"

"Those pink eyes!"

"What a dream!"

"But not for you, pal."

"What's he got that I haven't got?"

"A crown of light, buddy, that's what."

"Oh, what do I care? There are plenty of other fish in the sea," one said, and he went off shrugging his spines.

Discreetly followed by Professor Duck and Dr. Dandy-Green, Max hurried through the Park, looking for Bianca.

I got off to a bad start last night, he said to himself. *I was too pushy, and, anyway, she didn't like all that stuff about being King. I have to sweet-talk her. Flattery never fails, they say.*

When he did, at last, find the albino sow, she was making her way from the Lily Pond to the Ornamental Gardens. Max hid himself and his light until she had gone by. It had occurred to him that it would be a good idea to bring her a present, and at that moment luck was with him.

A slithering sound alerted him, and then he saw the curving shape of a small grass snake, winding its way through a flower border.

Max ran forward. With one bite he killed the snake, and then, carrying its still wriggling body in his mouth, he hurried after the albino.

"Hello, Bianca!" cried Max with his mouth full. Dropping the snake in front of her, he added, "I've brought you a present."

Bianca turned, her pink eyes blinking in the flashes of blue light.

"Oh, it's you again," she said. "Are you looking for another bite on the nose, Your Majesty?"

"No, no," Max answered hurriedly. "It's just that I had to come and tell you how beautiful I think you are. I've never seen a hedgehog like you before."

"I don't suppose you have," said Bianca. "Thanks for the snake. And good-bye."

"But I want us to be . . . friends," said Max.

"No chance," said Bianca.

She bit off a large piece from the tail of the snake.

Max took a deep breath.

"Bianca," he said. "Will you marry me?"

"Not on your life," Bianca replied.

"But why not? What's wrong with me?"

Bianca swallowed her mouthful.

"Look, King Max or whatever your name is," she said. "Get this through your royal skull. I think you're a weirdo."

"What do you mean?" muttered the King of the Hedgehogs.

"Well, just take a look at yourself!" said Bianca. "Talk about freaks! With that stupid thing stuck on your head and that annoying blue light flashing all the time, you'd drive any girl up the wall. If that's what kings look like, give me a common or garden hedgehog every time."

10:22 P.M. Followed E.E. from Bandstand toward Lily Pond. Albino hedgehog sighted here. E.E. killed grass snake in flower border in Ornamental Gardens. Carried snake and presented it to albino. (Albino possibly female? Courtship behavior?)

10:31 P.M. Leaving albino to eat snake (tail first), E.E. returned to Lily Pond. At edge of pond, E.E. did not drink but appeared to be studying his own reflection in the water. After a while, E.E. moved slowly away from pond. Observation of E.E. discontinued (10:33 P.M.) in order to return to study albino's consumption of snake. Head of snake disappeared at 10:42 P.M.

With Bianca's words ringing in his ears, Max made his unhappy way to the Lily Pond. "Just take a look at yourself," she had said. He would. He did.

He stood at the rim of the pond and looked down at the still surface, seeing himself and his crown of light for the first time. Didn't he look every inch a king?

Yet she had called him a weirdo.

What should he do?

He did not want to give up his royal position. He liked being King Max the First.

But Bianca had said, "Give me a common or garden hedgehog every time." Bianca, whom he must make his bride, or he would die of a broken heart.

So there was no choice. His crown had to go. He had to get rid of it. But how?

He shook his head violently, but the transmitter was much too firmly attached, and no amount of rubbing it against trees or banging it against the ground shifted it an inch.

He was stuck with it. And because of it he would lose the love of his life.

At that moment, Max who had once thought himself a hodgeheg, Max the pioneer of road safety, Max the hero of hedgehogkind, Max the First, ruler of his people, became simply a most unhappy young hog who badly needed his mother's comfort, and he set off for home. His thoughts were in such a whirl that when he reached the road opposite Number 5A, he stepped right off the sidewalk without looking.

Chapter 7

In fact, he stepped right into the path of a large truck, which braked and stopped just in time.

Some humans are kind and some are cruel, and it so happened that the driver of this particular truck was the sort of person who would not hurt a fly, much less a hedgehog.

Now he climbed down from his cab and, blocking Max's further progress with one large boot, looked in amazement at what was before him.

"Who did that to you, old hog?" said the truck driver softly. "Kids, I guess, getting into mischief. I've heard of them tying tin cans to cats' tails. That's bad enough, but I've never seen anything like this before. A toy lighthouse stuck on a poor little hedgehog. What a trick to play! Never mind, pal. I'll get that off you soon enough."

He picked Max up by his crown and,

climbing back into his cab, got out his toolbox. One tap from a hammer and the flashing light flashed no more. One squeeze from a pair of pliers ensured that the transmitter would never again transmit. Then, very gently, so as not to hurt the tightly curled animal, the truck driver picked off, bit by bit, the rest of the device that had been so carefully glued on by Professor Duck and Dr. Dandy-Green, until at last Max was his old self again.

"There!" said the truck driver. "That's better."

He climbed down again, holding Max wrapped in a rag, and looked around. Across the road, he could see, were some houses with nice front lawns, and he walked toward them.

"Now then," he said, "you take some advice from me, old fella. Don't cross any more roads, you hear? There isn't a hedgehog in the world that has ever found a safe way to cross roads." With that, he pushed Max underneath the nearest garden gate. On it was its number—5A.

As the truck drove away, Max remained

rolled up in a ball, wondering what it was that some human had done to him now. When he uncurled, his eyes told him that the night was dark, just like nights used to be. No blue light flashed around him. Then his nose told him where he was. Then his ears heard the sound of shrill voices.

"Ma! Pa! Max has come home!" squeaked his three sisters.

In a moment, Max was surrounded by his family.

"Oh, Max!" Ma cried. "You've lost your crown!"

"Feels like it," said Max.

"Does that mean I'm no longer the mother of a king?"

"Looks like it," said Max.

"So we're not princesses?" wailed Peony, Pansy, and Petunia.

"Seems like it," said Max. "I'm just my old self again."

"Good," said Pa.

Uncle B. came hurrying through the hedge.

"Oh, Sire!" he gasped. "Whatever has befallen Your Majesty?"

"I'm not my majesty anymore, Uncle B.," Max said. "And by the way, I'm very sorry I was so rude to you the other evening."

"Good," said Pa.

"Oh, that's quite all right, Your . . . I mean, Max," said Uncle B.

He sounded depressed at this abrupt end to his dreams.

"Cheer up, B.," said Pa. "It looks like this is the first and last time anyone is going to believe that story about a King of the Hedgehogs."

Uncle B. sighed deeply.

"In fact," chuckled Pa, "you might say that King Max the First is also King Max the Last."

"Never mind, Max dear," said Ma. "You'll always be a king in my eyes."

That's what I came home for, thought Max, *to be comforted by my mom.*

And why did I need comforting?

Because Bianca didn't like me.

And why didn't she like me?

Because I had all that stuff on my head.

But I haven't got it anymore!

"Thanks, Ma," he said. "And now I must be going. I have to meet someone."

"A girl!" cried Peony, Pansy, and Petunia with one voice.

"Someone special, Max dear?" asked Ma.

"Yes," said Max. "Very special."

"Thinking of settling down, are you?" asked Pa.

"Yes, Pa," said Max. "If she'll have me."

"Well, take my advice, son," said Pa. "Always agree with everything she says. That's what I've always done with your mother."

"Oh, Pa!" squeaked Ma. "The things you say!"

"I hope you have good fortune, Max," said Uncle B.

As Max slipped under the gate, he could hear them all wishing him well.

"Good luck, Max," they cried. "Good luck!"

♛

Because of Bianca's color, Max found her quite easily. She was by herself in the children's playground in one corner of the Park, hunting for woodlice.

Max did not approach her directly but nosed the ground as though he, too, were hunting. He watched her all the while out of the corner of his eye, thinking how lovely she looked.

Gradually he moved nearer until he was within speaking distance. Then, politely, he said, "Good morning."

I suppose she'll say, "Oh, it's you again," he

thought. *Or maybe she'll give me another bite.*

But Bianca looked up and answered, "Good morning!" in what sounded like a pleased voice.

She doesn't recognize me! thought Max.

"Do you know," said Bianca, "that you're the first boy who's spoken to me for days? Females have been quite polite to me, and one or two old boars, but you're the first young male to say a word to me. All the rest just turned and ran as soon as they saw me coming. I can't think why."

I can, said Max to himself. *King's orders.*

"Anyone would think I had bad breath or smelled awful or something," said Bianca. "I haven't, have I? I don't, do I?"

"No, certainly not," said Max. "Your breath is as sweet as the night breeze, and you smell of wildflowers."

At this speech, Bianca looked more carefully at him with her poor-sighted pink eyes.

"Your voice is familiar," she said. "Do I know you?"

"My name is Victor Maximilian St. George," Max replied.

"That's a mouthful," said Bianca. "Do people call you that?"

"No. Just Max."

"Funny," said Bianca. "I met another boar called Max recently. It must be a common name around here."

"What was he like, this other Max?" asked Max.

"A real bighead," said Bianca. "He called himself the King of the Hedgehogs, if you can believe that. He wore a thing on his head with a flashing light on it. Talk about a show-off! He was totally in love with himself. But I told him off, that's for sure."

Max wrinkled his nose.

"I'll bet you did," he answered. "He sounds terrible. I'm not like that at all. I'm just a common or garden hedgehog."

"Oh, I wouldn't say that," murmured Bianca.

Max gulped.

"What would you say?" he asked.

"I'd say you were quite a good-looking boy," the albino sow replied. "By the way, my name's Bianca."

"Oh," said Max.

"Do you like woodlice?"

"Yes."

"Have one of mine."

"Thanks," said Max. "Do you think . . . can . . . could . . . would . . . do you think we could meet again? Go for a walk perhaps?"

"I don't see why not," said Bianca.

Chapter 8

"I'm afraid we've lost him," said Professor Duck.

"Looks like it," Dr. Dandy-Green agreed.

The two scientists were sitting in their laboratory a few days later.

For several nights now, they had searched the Park from end to end and explored all the suburban gardens, but without success.

"Even if his light had failed," said Dr. Dandy-Green, "the transmitter should have been working. But we haven't picked up any signal at all."

"We have to face the fact," said Professor Duck, "that E.E. is no longer with us. He might have moved to another territory, I suppose, but I think it's much more likely he's shared the fate of so many hedgehogs."

"He's been run over, you mean?" asked the doctor.

"Yes."

"But he was so careful. You remember that time we saw him crossing the road? Anyone would think he'd learned the road safety rules. It's extraordinary, really, the things we've observed."

"Yes. There was that road crossing, and then all the other hedgehogs lining up to be inspected by him."

"And the way they all followed him around the Park."

"And that huge crowd that surrounded him in the Bandstand the second time, as though he were making a speech to them."

"We may have lost him," said Dr. Dandy-Green, "but think of what we've gained— enough material to write a revolutionary paper about the behavior of *Erinaceus*

europaeus. No one has ever witnessed such scenes before."

"We'll amaze the scientific world," said Professor Duck.

"And we should mention the albino in our report," said Dr. Dandy-Green. "It's quite a rare find among hedgehogs."

The professor sighed.

"Yes," he said. "If indeed it was a sow, I just wish it could have paired off with our friend E.E. They'd have made a nice couple."

Even as the two men talked, Max and Bianca were eating breakfast together in the Ornamental Gardens. It had been a wet night, and the rain had brought out a feast of slugs and snails as usual. They squatted side by side, the handsome young boar and the beautiful young sow, their jaws working rhythmically.

After a while Max spoke.

"You know that boy you were telling me about—the one with all that stuff on his head?"

"Yes," said Bianca. "He called himself King Max the First. Isn't that crazy?"

King Max the Last, thought the ex-monarch.

"What else did he say to you?" he went on.

"He asked me to marry him!" said Bianca. "What nerve! And just suppose I liked him—which I most certainly did not—imagine what our babies would have looked like! Half of them would probably have been born with flashing blue lights on their heads."

Max took a deep breath.

"Our babies wouldn't be like that, Bianca," he said.

Bianca swallowed the snail she was eating and looked directly at him.

"Victor Maximilian St. George," she said. "Are you asking me to marry you?"

"Yes," said Max. "Will you?"

"Yes," said Bianca. "I will."

About the Author

Dick King-Smith has been a farmer and a teacher as well as an award-winning author of children's books. His book *Babe: The Gallant Pig* was adapted into the hugely successful movie *Babe.*

Mr. King-Smith lives in Gloucestershire, England, the place where he was born.

About the Illustrator

Brian Floca is the author and illustrator of *The Frightful Story of Harry Walfish,* and he is the illustrator of *Mixed-Up Max* and *Jenius: The Amazing Guinea Pig,* both by Dick King-Smith. Mr. Floca also illustrated *Poppy* by Avi (winner of the 1996 *Boston Globe-Horn Book* Award for fiction) and *Luck with Potatoes* (a *Boston Globe* "Best of '95" children's book).

Mr. Floca lives and works in New York City.

Also by Dick King-Smith

The Hedgehog family of Number 5A wants to go to the park across the street, but the traffic makes it impossible to cross safely. Young Max has noticed that humans seem to get across the road quite easily, so he sets out to discover their secret. Dick King-Smith's unique humor is displayed throughout this wonderful tale of a little hedgehog who solves a very big problem.

ISBN 0-8167-4437-8

Available wherever you buy books.